MOUSE LOVES SNOW

by Lauren Thompson

illustrated by Buket Erdogan

Ready-to-Read

Simon Spotlight

New York   London   Toronto   Sydney   New Delhi

To Robert and Owen—L. T.

To the peacefulness that snow brings, and to a
peaceful world.—B. E.

SIMON SPOTLIGHT
An imprint of Simon & Schuster Children's Publishing Division
1230 Avenue of the Americas, New York, New York 10020
This Simon Spotlight edition November 2017
Text copyright © 2005 by Lauren Thompson
Illustrations copyright © 2005 by Buket Erdogan
Manufactured in the United States of America 1017 LAK
10 9 8 7 6 5 4 3 2 1
Cataloging-in-Publication Data for this title is available from the Library of Congress.
ISBN 978-1-5344-0181-5 (pbk)
ISBN 978-1-5344-0182-2 (hc)
ISBN 978-1-5344-0183-9 (eBook)

This book was previously published, with slightly different text,
as *Mouse's First Snow*.

Look!

It is snowing!

Snow is all around.

Mouse and Poppa
go out to play.

Poppa slides
down the hill.

Woosh,
swoosh!

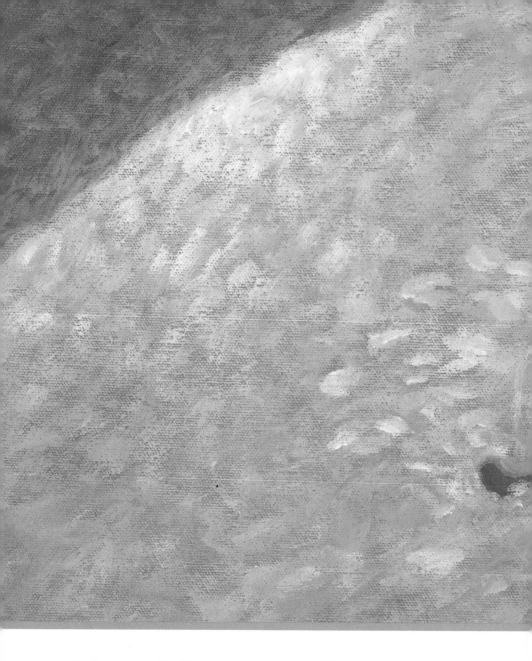

Now Mouse will try.
Pliff,

ploof!

Good job, Mouse!

Poppa skates
across the ice.

Zippity,

zip!

Now Mouse will try.
Twirly,

whirly!

Good job, Mouse!

Poppa makes angel
wings in the snow.

Swish,

whish!

Now Mouse will try.

Flap,

flop!

Good job, Mouse!

Poppa builds a grand
snow house.

Push,

pile!

Now Mouse will try.

Pitty,

pat!

Good job, Mouse!

Poppa rolls
a round snowball.

Tumble,
rumble!

Now Mouse will try.

Roly,

poly!

Good job, Mouse!

Then, Poppa climbs
up high.

Tipsy,

topsy!

Pick,

peg,

poke!

Surprise! A frosty
little snow mouse.

Just like Mouse!

Mouse loves snow!